Text
copyright © 2010
by Samantha Davis

Illustrations
copyright © 2010
by Sophie Fatus

All rights reserved / CIP Data is available.
Published in the United States 2010 by
🍎 Blue Apple Books,
515 Valley St. Maplewood, NJ 07040
www.blueapplebooks.com
First Edition Printed
in China
09/10

ISBN 978-1-60905-044-3

2 4 6 8 10 9 7 5 3 1

Distributed in the U.S. by Chronicle Books

by Samantha Davis ♥ illustrated by Sophie Fatus

BEAR
in
Love

Blue Apple Books

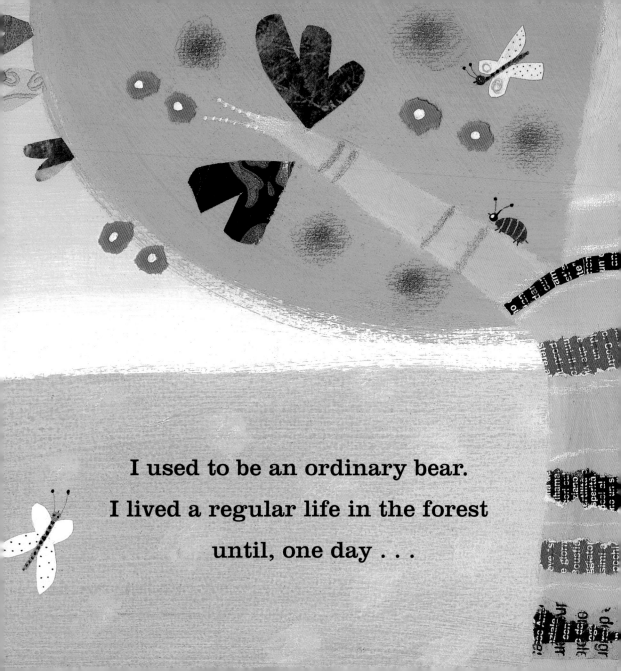

I used to be an ordinary bear.
I lived a regular life in the forest
until, one day . . .

I fell in love
with a bunny!

My regular life in the forest
is no longer regular.

My love is a secret.

No one knows
how I feel.

I watch bunny from a distance—
too scared to get close.

I imagine what we could do together.

In winter we could be skating partners.

In spring
we could ride bikes.

In summer we could have picnics.

In fall we could throw leaves and shout:

But Bunny doesn't know I exist.

I need to make myself known.

But how?

Should I send flowers?

Should I leave
a basket of goodies?

Or should I sing
and dance?

Right now,
I'm watching how Bunny's nose
twitches and wiggles.

It moves to the left,
then moves to the right.
Amazing!

I am getting ready
to approach her
and say how I feel.

Suddenly Bunny runs off,

scared and frightened.

Wait!

Don't run away!

I need to talk to you!

I catch up with Bunny.

I blurt out

what I've been holding inside:

Can we be

friends?

Bunny listens.

I don't hear
"YES."

But I don't hear "NO" either.

Bunny thinks I'm okay.

Bunny likes me!

Bunny wants to hang out!

Now . . .

next spring . . .

next summer . . .

and maybe forever!